D0376823

THE GHOST IN THE
FIRST ROW

created by
GERTRUDE CHANDLER WARNER

Illustrated by Robert Papp

ALBERT WHITMAN & Company
Morton Grove, IL

The Ghost in the First Row
Created by Gertrude Chandler Warner;
Illustrated by Robert Papp.

ISBN 13: 978-0-8075-5566-8 (hardcover)
ISBN 13: 978-0-8075-5567-5 (paperback)

Cover art by Robert Papp.

For information about Albert Whitman & Company,
visit our web site at www.albertwhitman.com.

Contents

THE GHOST IN THE
FIRST ROW

CHAPTER 1

Lady Chadwick's Riddle

"Is it really haunted, Grandfather?" asked six-year-old Benny, his eyes huge.

"Haunted?" James Alden looked puzzled, but only for a moment. "Oh, I suppose you children heard me on the phone?"

Jessie poured more milk into Benny's glass. "Yes, you were talking to Aunt Jane about the Trap-Door Theater, Grandfather," she explained. At twelve, Jessie often acted like a mother to her younger brother and sister.

Violet, who was ten, looked up. "Benny

heard you say it was haunted, Grandfather."

Fourteen-year-old Henry shook his head. "Ghosts don't exist, Benny," he said. He sounded very sure.

The four Alden children—Henry, Jessie, Violet, and Benny—were sitting around the dining room table with their grandfather. They were discussing their upcoming visit to nearby Elmford. Aunt Jane had invited the children to stay with her while Uncle Andy was away on business.

Grandfather put down his fork. "The Trap-Door Theater was closed years ago, Benny," he explained. "Sometimes people start talking about ghosts when a building's been empty for a long time."

"That's true," said Mrs. McGregor, as she came into the room. "It's been called the haunted theater for as long as I can remember." She placed a bowl of salad on the table. "From what I've heard, they've done a wonderful job fixing up the old place."

Grandfather nodded. "That building was quite an eyesore," he said. "Now it looks just like it did when it was first built in the late 1800s."

"Aunt Jane bought tickets for opening night," Violet told their housekeeper, her eyes shining. "We'll be seeing a mystery play."

"And mysteries are our specialty!" added Benny, sounding just as excited as his sister. There was nothing the children loved better than a mystery, and together they'd managed to solve quite a few.

"I bet you'll have that mystery figured out before the last act, Benny," guessed Mrs. McGregor.

"Well, I am very good at sniffing out clues," Benny admitted.

Henry couldn't help laughing. "Benny, you're almost as good at sniffing out clues as you are at sniffing out food!"

"Right!" Benny gave his brother the thumbs-up sign. The youngest Alden was known for his appetite. He was always hungry.

"Aunt Jane had a hunch you'd enjoy a good whodunit," said Grandfather, as Mrs. McGregor walked out of the room.

"A what?" Benny looked puzzled.

"A whodunit," Henry repeated. "That's another name for a mystery, Benny."

"Oh, I get it," said Benny, catching on. "They call it a whodunit because you figure out who did it. Right?"

"Right," said Grandfather, as he passed the salad along. "And the play's supposed to be a first-rate whodunit. At least, that's what Aunt Jane tells me."

"One thing's for sure," said Jessie. "It'll be great to see Aunt Jane again."

"I'll second that!" Henry said.

"Yes, it's been a while since you've had a visit." Grandfather helped himself to the mashed potatoes.

Just then, Watch ran over, wagging his tail.

"Sorry, Watch," Violet said, petting their family dog softly on the head. "You can't go with us this time."

"Dogs aren't allowed on the train," said Benny.

"Besides," put in Violet, "you need to keep Grandfather and Mrs. McGregor company while we're gone."

"And look after our boxcar," added Henry.

After their parents died, the four Alden children had run away. For a while, their home was an old boxcar in the woods. But then their grandfather, James Alden, had found them. He brought his grandchildren to live with him in his big white house in Greenfield. Even the boxcar was given a special place in the backyard. The children often used it as a clubhouse.

"I'll drop you off at the train station after lunch tomorrow," said Grandfather. "Aunt Jane will be waiting for you when you arrive in Elmford."

"Thanks, Grandfather," said Jessie. "We'll pack tonight, then we won't be rushed in the morning."

The other Aldens smiled at each other. They could always count on Jessie to be organized.

Violet was wondering about something.

"Grandfather, why was the Trap-Door Theater left empty for such a long time?"

"Well, when the theater was first built, Violet," said Grandfather, "it was Elmford's pride and joy. Tickets were always sold out. But as the years went by, the building needed repairs. It slowly became more and more run-down. Soon people didn't want to go there anymore."

"Why didn't they do the repairs?" Benny wondered.

"The town of Elmford didn't have the money, Benny. The council finally closed the theater down."

"How did they finally get the money to fix it up?" Jessie wondered.

"When Alice Duncan died, she left her money to the town to restore the place" said Grandfather. "Alice was one of Aunt Jane's neighbors."

"What a wonderful thing to do!" said Violet. Jessie nodded. "She saved the old theater."

"For now, anyway." Grandfather put down his fork. "Everyone's hoping the theater will bring tourists into town. But . . . "

"If it doesn't," guessed Henry, "they'll

close it down again?"

"I'm afraid so, Henry. But if the theater brings tourists into town, it'll be good for everyone."

"That makes sense," Henry said after a moment's thought. "There'll be more shoppers going in and out of the stores. Right, Grandfather?"

"Right." Grandfather nodded.

"Oh, I'm sure the play will be a success," said Violet.

Benny was quick to agree. "Everybody likes a mystery!"

* * * *

True to her word, Aunt Jane was waiting for the Aldens when their train pulled into Elmford the next day.

"I brought my binoculars for the play, Aunt Jane!" Benny shouted, running up and giving her a hug. Laughing, Aunt Jane returned the hug.

"Don't worry, Benny," she said. "We'll be sitting in the first row. I don't think you'll need binoculars."

"We can't wait to see what the theater

looks like now," Violet said.

Henry loaded the suitcases into the car and they all got inside.

"Actually, you can take a peek at it right away," Aunt Jane said. "The theater is just around the corner, so you can see it from the outside. It's been completely done over."

"Thanks to your neighbor," said Henry, sitting up front beside Aunt Jane. "Alice Duncan, I mean."

"Yes, Alice was a great fan of the theater," said Aunt Jane. "And a wonderful friend."

Violet didn't like to hear the note of sadness in Aunt Jane's voice. She was trying to think of something cheery to say, but Jessie spoke first.

"I bet Alice would be pleased with all the work that's been done," she said.

"Yes, I think she would." Aunt Jane smiled at Jessie through the rearview mirror. "In the old days, Alice had a seat in the first row for every mystery play. And she always brought her knitting and a bag of popcorn with her for intermission."

"Wow," said Benny. "I guess Alice liked mysteries."

"She sure did, Henry." Aunt Jane nodded. "As a matter of fact, she even wrote her own mystery plays."

The children were surprised to hear this.

"Alice Duncan was a writer?" Jessie asked.

"She sure was," said Aunt Jane. "Whenever we had a cup of tea together, she'd tell me about her latest codes and clues."

That sounded like fun to Benny. "I bet she was a good writer."

"The best, Benny," said Aunt Jane. "And she always put a surprise twist in the last act."

"Were any of her plays performed in the Trap-Door Theater?" Jessie wondered.

"It was always Alice's dream to have one of her plays performed." Aunt Jane sighed. "But sadly, her dream never came true."

"What a shame!" said Violet.

"Alice wanted to give other writers the chance she never had," Aunt Jane went on. "That's why she left her money to the town—

on one condition."

At this, the children were curious. "What was the condition?" Henry wondered.

"That a contest be held every summer. The winner would get a cash award," said Aunt Jane, "and the winning play would be performed at the Trap-Door Theater."

"Cool!" said Benny.

"The winner this year is a local college student, Tricia Jenkins. And from what I hear, she can really use the money."

"Oh?" Henry asked.

"Yes, apparently Tricia's putting herself through school," Aunt Jane told them. "She earns extra money working at her computer. They say she's an expert typist."

"So, it's Tricia's play we'll be seeing on opening night?" Jessie wondered.

"Yes." Aunt Jane nodded. "And I'm really looking forward to it. The judges were all very impressed that someone so young could write such a fine play."

"Then it's bound to be a big hit," Henry concluded.

"We're keeping our fingers crossed, Henry. Nobody wants the theater to close down again," said Aunt Jane.

"Well, guess what, Aunt Jane?" Benny piped up. "I'm going to clap extra hard at the end of the play—just in case."

"In case what, Benny?" asked Henry, looking over his shoulder.

"In case the theater really *is* haunted," said Benny. "The clapping will drown out all the booing from the ghosts."

"That's a good one, Benny," Henry said, as everyone burst out laughing.

CHAPTER 2

The Haunted Theater

The Aldens drew in their breath as they pulled up in front of the Trap-Door Theater.

"Oh, it looks wonderful!" said Violet, as they climbed out of the car. She gazed admiringly at the stone building with its marble columns.

Henry let out a low whistle. "Awesome."

Aunt Jane looked pleased. "See those stone lions on either side of the ticket window? We thought they were lost forever," she said.

"But then, one of the workmen came across them in a dark corner of the basement."

"That was lucky," said Benny.

"Yes, they were quite a find," Aunt Jane said, with a big smile. "Now the theater looks just like it did when it was first built."

"They really did a great job," said Jessie.

Aunt Jane agreed. "It's like stepping back in time," she said. "In fact, the mayor's planning to arrive by horse and buggy on opening night."

Henry's eyebrows shot up. "Wow, he's really getting into the spirit of things."

"Oh, yes," said Aunt Jane. "This is the biggest thing that's happened to Elmford in a long time."

Benny tilted his head back to look up at the sign above the doorway. "What does that say?" he wanted to know. The youngest Alden was just learning to read.

Jessie read the words on the billboard aloud. *"Lady Chadwick's Riddle*—Starring Fern Robson."

"You're not throwing your money away on

tickets, are you?" Everyone whirled around as a middle-aged man with a mustache walked towards them. He was wearing a business suit, and his dark hair was slicked back.

"Hello, Gil," Aunt Jane greeted him. "We were just checking out the theater." She introduced the children to Gil Diggs, the owner of the local movie theater.

"If you ask me, Alice wasted her money on this place."

Aunt Jane stared at Gil in surprise. "I think the Trap-Door Theater does the town proud."

"It's just a matter of time before they close it down again," Gil said, shaking his head. As he walked away, he called back over his shoulder, "Mark my words!"

"He doesn't seem very happy about the theater," said Benny.

"Gil has a lot on his mind these days," Aunt Jane explained. "It makes him seem a bit grumpy sometimes. You see, his movie theater hasn't been doing well lately."

Violet asked, "Why's that, Aunt Jane?"

"They opened a huge movie complex on the highway, Violet. Some of Gil's customers go there now. And on top of that, a lot of people would rather rent movies and watch them at home these days."

"That's true," said Henry. "We do that, too."

Aunt Jane nodded. "I imagine Gil thinks the Trap-Door Theater will take away even more business. He doesn't seem to understand," she said, "that a successful theater will bring tourists into town."

"And that would be good for everyone's business," finished Henry, remembering what Grandfather had said.

"Exactly," said Aunt Jane. "But it'll take time for Gil to realize that, I'm afraid. Speaking of time," she added, "I'd better take Uncle Andy's watch to the jewelry store for repairs. I'll be right back."

While the children were waiting, they noticed a young woman in a hooded white top and track pants step out of the theater. She was wearing sunglasses, and her coppery red hair was pulled back into a ponytail. A tall man appeared seconds later, the sleeves of his white shirt rolled up above his elbows, and a pencil stuck behind his ear.

From where they were standing, the Aldens couldn't help overhearing their conversation.

"Hold on a minute," the young man was saying. "You're getting upset over nothing, Fern."

"How can you call it nothing? I have a good mind to walk out on—"

The man broke in, "I'm sure it's just somebody's idea of a joke."

"Well, if it's a joke," the woman shot back, "it's not a very funny one!"

"Her name is Fern," Henry whispered to the others. "She must be the actress starring in the play."

Jessie felt uncomfortable listening to the conversation. "Maybe we should walk over to the jewelry store," she suggested in a low voice. "It isn't nice to eavesdrop."

"Oh, here comes Aunt Jane now," said Violet.

"Jane Bean!" The young man waved a hand

in the air as Aunt Jane approached. "You're just the person I wanted to see."

Aunt Jane introduced the children to Ray Shaw. He was the director of the Trap-Door Theater. Then she said, "What can I do for you, Ray?"

"I was hoping I could stop by tonight," said Ray, "to pick up a few things from your shed."

"Of course!" Aunt Jane nodded. Then she turned to the children. "Alice left most of her belongings to the theater," she explained. "We're keeping them in the old shed out back."

"The workmen should be finished in the basement soon," said Ray. "Then we'll have a dry place to keep all the stage props."

"That's good," Aunt Jane told him. "As you know, the lock's been broken on that shed for years."

Ray laughed. "I don't think anybody would be interested in stealing old furniture," he told her.

"By the way," Aunt Jane added, "how are rehearsals going?"

"Don't ask!" The woman with the coppery red hair came over and joined their group. "I'm at the end of my rope."

Ray introduced everyone to Fern Robson who was playing the lead in Lady Chadwick's Riddle.

"This theater makes my hair stand on end," Fern went on, shivering a little. "I'm a bundle of nerves!"

Henry and Jessie exchanged glances. Why was Fern so upset?

"I have an idea," said Aunt Jane. "Why don't you both join us for dinner this evening? How does a barbecue sound?"

"Sounds great!" said Ray. "Count me in."

"Me, too," said Fern. "I could use a break from the ghost world." The actress shivered a little.

The Aldens looked at one another. *The ghost world?* What on earth was Fern Robson talking about?

CHAPTER 3

Goose Bumps

"Fern is such a pretty name," Aunt Jane was saying, as they sat around the picnic table in the backyard.

"Oh, do you like it?" Fern's face broke into a smile. "You know, I couldn't make up my mind between Fern and Cassandra. But I decided to go with Fern."

Benny wrinkled up his forehead. "You named yourself?"

"Well, I'm really Susan. But I wanted a name with more pizzazz. Something that would look good up in lights."

"I think you made a great choice," Violet said.

"Thank you, Violet," said Fern. "Lots of people in show business change their names, you know. Even the winner of the play-writing contest changed her name. Isn't that true, Ray?"

Ray wiped some mustard from the corner of his mouth. "Well, she changed her nick-name, at least."

"I was hoping to see my name first on the billboard," Fern went on. "Above the title of the play, I mean." She shot the director a look. "But I suppose that was hoping for too much."

Ray rolled his eyes, but he didn't say any-thing. Instead, he dished up another helping of potato salad.

Jessie couldn't help noticing that the Fern had hardly eaten a bite. She was only poking at her food with a fork.

The actress caught Jessie's look. "I'm afraid I have a nervous stomach," she said. "I can't stop thinking about all the strange things that have been happening at the theater."

Aunt Jane looked up in surprise. "What's been happening?"

Fern leaned forward and whispered, "The ghosts have been acting up."

"This isn't the time or the place—" Ray began.

Fern waved that away. "They've been using it for years, you know. It gives me goose bumps just to think about it!"

"What do you mean?" Benny's big eyes were round.

"I'm talking about the ghosts." Fern replied. "They've been using the theater to perform their plays."

The Aldens looked at one another. They were too stunned to speak.

"The ghosts aren't happy about the theater opening up again," Fern went on. "They don't want to share it with the public."

"You don't really believe that," said Henry. "Do you, Fern?"

"Take a look at the facts," Fern said.

Jessie stared at the actress. "What facts?"

"Well, for starters, things keep disappearing." Fern looked slowly around the table. "Then they show up in the oddest places."

"That's weird," said Benny. He was so interested in the conversation that he still hadn't taken a bite of his hamburger.

"Remember Lady Chadwick's hat?" Fern turned to look at Ray. "The one with the yellow marigolds on it?"

"I remember," said Ray. "We found it hanging from the chandelier in the lobby."

"What's a chandelier?" Benny wanted to know.

"It's a fancy ceiling light," Henry explained.

Violet giggled. She couldn't help it—it seemed so funny. "Well, if it's a ghost," she said, "it's a ghost with a sense of humor."

Everyone laughed—except Fern. "This isn't a laughing matter," she said with a frown. "The ghosts aren't happy."

"Now, Fern—" Ray started to say.

"It's no use shaking your head, Ray. You know it's true. And now Alice Duncan has joined the ghostly audience."

"*What?*" Aunt Jane almost choked on her lemonade.

"What makes you say that?" Jessie asked.

Fern leaned forward again. "One morning, we found a ball of yarn and some knitting needles on a seat in the first row."

Ray added, "We even found some popcorn on the floor."

"And as everybody knows," Fern said, "Alice always brought her knitting and a bag of popcorn to the theater with her. It was mentioned in all the newspaper articles after she died."

"But Alice wanted the theater opened up to the public again," Jessie pointed out. "Didn't she?"

Violet nodded. "That's why she left her money to the town."

"I guess she changed her mind." Fern suddenly pushed her plate away. "My stomach is too upset to eat. I'd better go home and lie down."

"Why don't you take the morning off

tomorrow, Fern," Ray suggested. "We'll postpone the rehearsal until after lunch."

"I just might take you up on that," Fern said. "I need my beauty sleep." With that, she said good-bye and left.

Ray apologized for Fern's behavior. "She can be a handful sometimes. But she really is a wonderful actress."

"I can understand why Fern would be upset with so many strange things happening at the theater," said Aunt Jane. "I wonder who's responsible for all those pranks."

Jessie asked, "Did you notice anyone hanging around, Ray?"

"Only the actors and the stagehands." The director shook his head. "Nobody else."

"Are you sure?" Henry looked uncertain.

"Quite sure, Henry," said Ray. "We don't want anyone to see the theater until opening night."

Jessie had a thought. "What if somebody got in after everybody went home?"

Ray shook his head again. "I'm the only one with a key, Jessie."

"Maybe they didn't use a key," Benny suggested.

"I checked it out, Benny," Ray said. "It doesn't look like anyone broke in."

"Fern's right about one thing," said Violet. "If it's a joke, it's not a very funny one."

"No, it's not," Ray agreed. "It's making everyone in the cast and crew very nervous. Nobody wants to stay late anymore. They're all afraid of ghosts."

"You've sure got your work cut out for you, Ray," said Aunt Jane.

"You can say that again." Ray nodded. "I hired some high school kids to help with the posters, but they were a no-show. I have a hunch they were scared away by the rumors of ghosts."

"Maybe we could lend a hand," volunteered Henry.

"Of course," agreed Jessie, while Violet and Benny nodded.

"Really?" Ray looked surprised—and pleased.

"We'd like to help," Violet said shyly.

Ray looked at the Aldens' eager faces.

"Putting up posters around town is hard work," he warned them.

Aunt Jane laughed. "Oh, you don't know these children, Ray. There's nothing they like better than hard work."

"Well, I'd be very grateful for your help," Ray told them. "We need all the advertising we can get. I've been trying to get someone from the local paper to do a write-up. But . . . they're not interested unless it'll grab the readers' attention."

"Well, we'll help for sure," promised Benny. "When do we start?"

Ray was all smiles. "How does first thing in the morning sound?"

The Aldens thought it sounded just fine. After dinner, they walked over to the shed with Ray. Stepping inside, they found it overflowing with tables, chairs, trunks, and wooden boxes.

"Alice sure had lots of stuff," Benny said, looking around.

"She sure did," said Ray. "And we plan to make good use of it on stage."

Violet was taking a close look at an old typewriter. "Grandfather has one just like this in the attic."

"The keys stick and it won't print *w* at all," Ray told her. "But Alice used that old typewriter for years and years."

"She never used a computer?" Henry asked.

"Never. Not even when her fingers got weaker as she got older," said Ray. "She couldn't peck away at the typewriter keys anymore, but she still refused to use a computer. Instead, she recorded her plays on tape and hired a college student to type them up for her." Ray lifted the lid of a wooden box. "See? Alice's tapes are right here."

"The box is almost full," Benny noted.

Just then, Ray spotted a book on the windowsill. Reaching for it, he began to flip through the pages. "Looks like Alice's appointment book," he said. "Your aunt Jane's mentioned in here quite a bit."

"They were good friends," Jessie said.

"Alice's last entry seems to be about shoes."

Ray read the words aloud: *Shoe won't fit. Tell P.J. to make change.*

"I guess Alice bought a pair of shoes that were too small," Henry figured.

"I think your aunt Jane might like this book," said Ray. "It would be a nice keepsake."

"We'll make sure she gets it," Jessie promised.

Ray glanced around. "Now, there's something I can use!" He reached a bag down from a shelf. The label read: *Plaster of Paris.*

"What will you use it for?" Benny wanted to know.

"A prop for the play," Ray said, as he poured half of the white powder into an empty container. "We need a plaster cast of a footprint." Then he added, "That's how Lady Chadwick proves the butler did it."

"You make the cast with powder?" asked Benny.

Ray nodded. "You mix plaster of Paris with water to form a paste," he said. "The paste hardens as it dries."

After helping Ray load up his pick-up

truck, the Aldens said good-bye, then headed back to the house.

"I wish we could figure out what's going on with the ghosts," said Violet.

"We'll get to the bottom of it," Benny said. "Right, Henry?"

"I hope so," said Henry. "I'm just not sure how."

CHAPTER 4

In the Spotlight

It was after midnight when Benny awoke to the sound of thunder. He slid out of bed and tiptoed across the room to shut the window. As he peered out into the rainy night, something caught his eye. Was that the beam of a flashlight sweeping back and forth across the backyard?

Henry stirred. "Benny?" he asked sleepily. "What's going on?"

"Somebody's out there," Benny answered in a hushed voice.

Henry came up behind him. "Your eyes must be sharper than mine," he said. "I can't see anybody."

Benny looked at his brother. "Someone just went into the shed."

"I doubt there's anyone out there, Benny."

"But I saw something moving, Henry."

Henry put an arm around his brother. "It's easy to imagine all kinds of things on a dark and stormy night."

Benny shivered in his pajamas. "Don't you think—"

"I think we should get back into our warm beds," said Henry.

Benny nodded. But he knew he had seen someone.

* * * *

"Ray says putting up posters is hard work," Benny said the next morning. He was cracking eggs into a bowl. "We'll need a big breakfast."

"Well, you do have a big appetite, Benny," teased Henry, who was keeping an eye on the bacon sizzling on the stove.

"Something sure smells good," Aunt Jane said, as she came into the kitchen.

"We're making breakfast." Jessie placed a platter of toast on the table. "We wanted to surprise you, Aunt Jane."

"Speaking of surprises," said Henry, "we forgot all about Alice's appointment book."

"Alice's what?" asked Aunt Jane.

"Ray came across Alice's appointment book in the shed," Jessie explained as Henry raced outside. "He thought you should have it as a keepsake."

Henry was back in a flash, waving the appointment book in the air. While he was removing his muddy shoes, Violet noticed something slip from the pages and flutter to the floor. She hurried to pick it up.

"Looks like an ad torn from a newspaper," she said.

"Oh?" Aunt Jane raised an eyebrow. "What does it say, Violet?"

Violet read the ad aloud: *Typist available. Reasonable rates. Ask for Patty at 894-8884.*

Aunt Jane nodded. "Patty must be the

college student Alice hired."

"To type the plays she recorded, right?" said Benny.

"Exactly!" said Aunt Jane, surprised that Benny knew this.

"You're mentioned in here a lot," Henry told his aunt, handing her the appointment book. "At least, that's what Ray says."

"Alice and I often got together for a cup of tea." Aunt Jane smiled a little. "She always had a pot of yellow marigolds on the table. Alice loved yellow marigolds, you know. She was always putting them in her plays."

"Lady Chadwick loves marigolds, too," said Benny.

"What do you mean?" Aunt Jane asked.

"Remember the hat they found hanging from the chandelier?" said Benny. "Lady Chadwick's hat, I mean. Fern said it had yellow marigolds on it."

"Hmm." Aunt Jane was only half-listening. She was busy leafing through the appointment book.

"Know what else, Aunt Jane?" Benny went

on, as he swallowed a mouthful of eggs. "Alice got a new pair of shoes, but they didn't fit. She wanted P.J. to take them back. Whoever that is."

"I thought I knew all of Alice's friends." Aunt Jane frowned. "I don't recall anyone with those initials." Putting the appointment book aside, she looked around at the children. "I guess you've got a busy day planned," she added, changing the subject.

Jessie nodded. "I can't wait to see the inside of the theater."

"The whole town's curious to see it," Aunt Jane said. "All the seats have sold out."

"That's great!" said Violet. "I knew everything would work out."

"The play runs all summer, Violet," Aunt Jane reminded her. "We can't be sure tickets will keep selling."

"One thing I don't understand," said Henry. "Even if they don't sell a lot of tickets, why would they close the theater down? It doesn't make sense when they just fixed it up."

"It costs a lot of money to produce plays,"

Aunt Jane explained. "The town can't afford to keep the theater going if tickets don't sell."

Benny, who was spreading honey on his toast, looked up. "Well, tickets won't sell if Fern quits."

Aunt Jane agreed. "Fern's a wonderful actress," she said. "It would be a disaster if she walks out on the play."

Violet frowned. "You don't think that's possible, do you, Aunt Jane?"

"There's no telling what Fern might do," Aunt Jane replied. "Especially if she thinks the theater's haunted."

"I wish we could do something to help," said Violet.

Aunt Jane smiled. "Putting posters up around town is a big help."

The children quickly finished breakfast, then set off for town on the bikes that Aunt Jane kept for them. When they reached the theater, Jessie noticed something different.

"Looks like Fern got her wish," she said, pointing to the billboard.

The others looked up at the sign. Fern's

name now appeared above the title of the play.

"Wow," said Benny. "I guess Ray really wants to keep her happy."

After leaving their bikes behind the theater, the Aldens made their way around to the front.

"I hope I didn't keep you waiting," Ray called out, as he hurried towards them. "I was having breakfast at the diner—with a reporter from the local paper."

"No problem," Henry said, as the director unlocked the theater door. "We just got here ourselves."

As they stepped inside, the children glanced admiringly at the fancy lobby with its red carpeting. Huge mirrors in gold frames covered the walls and a crystal chandelier hung from the ceiling.

"Ooooh!" cried Violet. "How beautiful!"

"Is that where you found Lady Chadwick's hat?" Benny pointed up at the light.

Ray nodded. "It still baffles me how it got up there."

"It sure is weird," said Jessie, as they followed the director to the far end of the lobby.

As Ray opened the oak doors that led into the auditorium, he suddenly took a step back in surprise. "What in the world?" he cried. "Somebody's been tampering with the lights."

Sure enough, a large standing spotlight was shining directly onto a seat in the first row of the theater! The Aldens could hardly believe their eyes.

Ray clicked his tongue. "Wait here, kids. I'll only be a minute."

As the director hurried backstage, Jessie said, "I wonder why the spotlight's pointed at the first row?"

"Let's check it out," Henry suggested. He headed down the aisle, the others close behind.

At the front of the theater, Benny's eyes widened. The others followed his gaze to where the circle of yellow light was shining on a seat in the front row—a seat that was littered with popcorn!

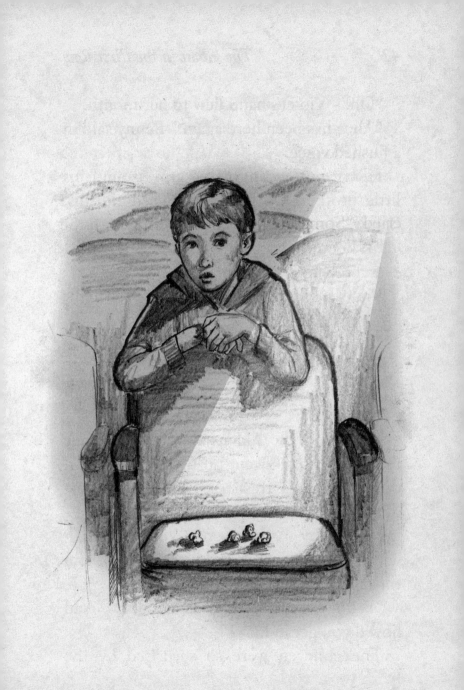

"Oh!" Violet's hand flew to her mouth.

"Alice has been here again," Benny said in a hushed voice.

Henry put a comforting arm around his little brother. "Anyone could've done this, Benny."

"Whoever it was," said Jessie, "they wanted everybody to notice."

Violet nodded. "They shone the spotlight right on to the seat."

"Let's clean this up before anybody else sees it," Jessie suggested.

Henry agreed. "Fern's nervous enough already."

With that, the Aldens set to work. They found a broom, swept up the popcorn, and threw it into a trash can. They were just finishing when they noticed someone standing close by. An attractive young woman with sandy-colored hair was watching them through narrowed eyes.

"Who are you?" she demanded. "And how'd you get in here?"

The children were so surprised by the

woman's harsh tone, they were speechless. Finally, Henry recovered his voice. "We're the Aldens," he said with a friendly smile. "I'm Henry. This is my brother, Benny, and my sisters, Violet and Jessie."

"We're putting posters up around town," Jessie added.

The young woman frowned. "The theater's off-limits to anyone but the cast and crew."

"But we're here to help," protested Benny.

"The last thing we need is a bunch of kids running around," the woman said. "This isn't a playground."

"That's true," said Jessie, who refused to be rude. "And we'll try not to bother you."

"Tricia!" Ray walked over, the rolled-up posters tucked under his arm. "What are you doing here so early? Rehearsal isn't for a few hours."

"I know," said Tricia. "But I was driving by and noticed the billboard out front. What's going on, Ray?"

Ray shifted uncomfortably. "Listen, Tricia—"

"No, you listen, Ray!" she cut in. "It's bad

enough my name's not even up there, but now *Fern's* name is above the title of my play?"

"Try to understand, Tricia," said Ray. "I'm just trying to keep Fern happy so she won't walk out."

"Who cares if she walks out?" demanded Tricia. "The understudy can play the part of Lady Chadwick, can't she?"

Benny whispered to Henry, "What's an—" But Henry knew the question before he asked it. "And understudy is somebody who goes on stage if an actor gets sick."

"Or quits," added Jessie.

"Fern wouldn't even have a role if it wasn't for me," Tricia was saying to Ray, her hands on her hips. "First she gets a bigger dressing room, then—"

Ray cut in. "That's enough, Tricia." His mouth was set in a thin, hard line. "I won't have you questioning my decisions."

With that, Tricia turned around and stomped out of the theater.

"Tricia's the winner of the playwriting contest," Ray explained to the children. "I'm afraid her nerves are a bit on edge. She's worried about opening night." He handed the posters to Henry. "There's more posters backstage, but these should keep you busy most of the day."

"We'll come back tomorrow and put up the rest," Jessie offered.

Ray looked surprised. "Are you sure you don't mind?"

The Aldens didn't mind at all. They were happy to do whatever they could to help.

"By the way," Ray added, as the children turned to go, "there's a tape recorder in the box with Alice's tapes. Would you mind bringing it along with you tomorrow? I promised Fern she could use it to practice her lines."

"No problem," said Jessie.

When they were outside the theater, Henry said, "Someone's working hard to make everyone believe there are ghosts in the theater."

"Why anyone would do such a thing?" Jessie wondered.

"You don't think—" Benny began.

"Are you wondering if the theater really is haunted?" Violet asked her little brother. "I don't blame you, Benny. I've been wondering that myself."

Henry shook his head. "A ghost didn't spill that popcorn."

"Now that I think about it," said Violet, "I'm sure there are no ghosts." She wasn't really sure, but she wanted Benny to believe she was.

All morning long the Aldens walked along the streets of Elmford, hanging posters up here, there, and everywhere. Finally, Benny plopped down on a park bench.

"Is it lunchtime yet?" he asked with a sigh.

Henry glanced at his watch. "Close enough," he said. "We could use a break."

Soon enough, the Aldens were sitting down to lunch at the local diner, studying the menus. When the waitress came over, Henry ordered a grilled cheese sandwich and a cola. Jessie had chicken on a bun, coleslaw and milk, and Violet ordered a toasted tomato sandwich and lemonade. Benny decided on a cheeseburger, fries, and chocolate milk.

While they waited for their food to arrive, the children turned their attention to the mystery. "Whoever is behind these pranks," said Jessie, "he—or she—sure knows a lot about Alice Duncan."

"That's true." Violet handed everyone a napkin from the shiny dispenser. "They know that Alice took her knitting and a bag of popcorn to the theater with her."

"And that she sat in the first row," added Benny.

"I'm sure most of Elmford knows that about Alice," said Henry.

As the waitress brought their food, Benny saw someone he knew. "Isn't that Gil Diggs?"

Sure enough, the owner of the local movie theater was sitting at a table in the corner. He was sipping coffee and talking on a cell phone.

"What choice do I have?" Gil was saying. "My business is going nowhere fast."

"He sure looks upset," Violet said, keeping her voice low.

"Yes, of course the whole thing makes me nervous." Gil was talking loudly now. "But I have to shut it down. That's all there is to it!"

"Uh-oh," whispered Benny. "Is Gil talking about the Trap-Door Theater?"

The Aldens looked at one another. None of them liked the sound of this.

CHAPTER 5

Whodunit?

When the Aldens returned to the theater, they found Ray outside by the back door. He was standing at an old table covered with tools and rags. The container filled with plaster of Paris was nearby. He looked over at the children and gave them a cheery smile.

"How did you make out?" he asked them.

"Good," Henry told him. "We found a spot for every poster."

Ray dried his hands on a rag. Then he

reached into his pocket and pulled out some dollar bills. "Let me pay you for—"

Jessie shook her head firmly. "Please put your money away, Ray."

"But . . . " he protested.

"We like to help," Violet said in her soft voice.

Ray hesitated for a moment. Then he shoved the dollar bills into his pocket again. "If you won't accept money, then at least accept my invitation to the dress rehearsal tomorrow night. We're having a potluck dinner for the cast and crew afterwards. I'd love to have you and your aunt join us."

"We'll check with Aunt Jane," said Jessie.

"But I'm pretty sure you can count us in."

"I hope so," said Ray, turning back to his work.

Benny was curious. "What are you making, Ray?"

"I'm making that mold of the butler's footprint, Benny. The stagehands are busy backstage, so I thought I'd do it myself."

"Super!" said Benny.

"I already made an impression of the butler's

shoe in the mud." Ray nodded towards a square container filled with dirt. "It's important to make the mold before the mud dries."

"Why's that?" Henry wondered.

"A footprint shrinks as the mud dries, Henry," Ray explained. "For the mold to fit the butler's shoe exactly, it has to be made while the dirt's still wet."

"That makes sense," said Henry.

The Aldens watched as the theater director stirred the plaster of Paris with water. When it was just the right thickness, he poured the mixture into the footprint.

"That should do it. Hopefully, the ghosts won't get at it before the plaster sets," Ray said with a wink.

Jessie caught Henry's eye. Was Ray joking—or did he really believe the theater was haunted?

* * * *

"Let's get that tape recorder for Ray before we forget," Jessie suggested, as they wheeled their bikes into Aunt Jane's driveway.

"Good idea," said Henry.

"Ray said it was in the box with Alice's tapes," Benny reminded them, following the others into the shed.

"That's funny," Violet said, looking around. "I'm sure it was right here on the table." Now there was nothing on the table but the old typewriter.

"I don't understand it," said Henry.

Jessie frowned. "What happened?"

"It was stolen," said Benny.

"Oh, Benny," said Jessie. "Who would steal Alice Duncan's tapes?"

"A thief, that's who!" Benny cried.

Henry looked over at his little brother. "You're thinking about last night, right?"

"I saw somebody out by the shed, Henry," Benny insisted. "I'm sure of it."

Jessie and Violet were surprised to hear this.

"But who would do such a thing?" Violet wondered. "And why?"

"Let's not say anything about the tapes," Henry suggested, "until we have a chance to do some investigating."

Over dinner, the Aldens took turns telling their aunt all about the latest prank. Violet finished by saying, "A spotlight was shining on a seat in the first row."

"I can't believe it!" Aunt Jane shook her head. "Those practical jokes won't seem very funny if they scare people away."

"Don't worry, Aunt Jane," said Benny. "We cleaned up the popcorn before anybody else could see it."

"That was good thinking, Benny," Aunt Jane told him, as she pushed her chair back.

"We'll do the dishes, Aunt Jane," Violet offered.

"Oh, thanks, Violet. It'll give me a chance to get some other work done." With that, Aunt Jane left the room.

"Maybe if we put our heads together," Jessie said, as she wrapped the leftover pasta, "we can get to the bottom of it."

But Violet wasn't so sure. "This is a tough mystery to figure out."

"Know what?" said Benny. "I think Alice's

tapes will show up again—in a strange place."

"What makes you say that?" Jessie asked her little brother.

"Remember what happened when Lady Chadwick's hat disappeared?" Benny reminded them. "They found it hanging from the chandelier in the lobby!"

Violet, who was filling the sink with soapy water, suddenly looked over. "You think the disappearing tapes is just another prank?"

"It's possible," Henry said thoughtfully.

Benny had an opinion about this. "I bet it is a trick," he said. "And I bet Gil Diggs is behind it."

"Gil's up to something, all right," said Henry. "I'm just not sure it has anything to do with the ghostly pranks."

"But we heard him on the phone," Benny argued. "Remember? He was talking about shutting it down."

"And the Trap-Door Theater *will* shut down," Violet pointed out, "if everybody's scared away by rumors of ghosts."

"You're forgetting something," Jessie said. "Gil doesn't have a key to the theater."

"That's true," said Henry. "Ray told us he has the only key."

"And he said there was no sign anyone broke in," Violet recalled.

"What if Gil is working with someone else?" Jessie suggested.

Henry hadn't thought of that. "There was somebody on the other end of that phone conversation," he admitted. "Maybe Gil knows somebody in the cast."

"Or the crew," added Benny.

Henry reached for a dishtowel. "Gil is afraid the Trap-Door Theater will take away even more customers," he admitted. "But he's not the only suspect."

"You're thinking about Tricia Jenkins, right?" said Jessie.

Benny looked puzzled. "Why would Tricia play tricks on everyone?"

"There's no reason for her to do something like that," said Violet.

"What if she's trying to get rid of Fern

Robson?" Henry suggested.

"By convincing her the theater's haunted?" asked Violet.

"We have to think of everything," Henry pointed out. "And Tricia doesn't seem to like Fern very much."

"She didn't seem very happy to see Fern's name on the billboard above the title," Jessie had to admit.

"It's not very nice to scare people." A frown crossed Benny's round face.

"No, it's not," agreed Violet, who was up to her elbows in soapy suds. "Fern's a nervous wreck."

"Maybe that's just what she wants everyone to believe," Jessie said. "Maybe she isn't nervous at all."

Henry turned to Jessie in surprise. "You think it's an act?"

"Could be," Jessie said, putting the clean plates into the cupboard. "It does seem to get her what she wants."

Henry added everything up on his fingers. "First she gets a bigger dressing room.

Then she gets to sleep in late."

"And don't forget about getting her name above the title," put in Jessie.

They had to admit it was possible. After all, Fern was an actress—and a good one. And wasn't Ray eager to keep her happy so she wouldn't quit?

"You really think Fern set up all those pranks just to get her own way?" Violet found it hard to believe.

Jessie shrugged. "Well, she seems to be able to wrap Ray around her little finger by acting frightened."

"It does seem that way," Violet said. But she didn't like to think Fern would do something so sneaky.

"Let's keep an eye on all of them," Henry suggested. "Gil, Tricia, and Fern."

Jessie suddenly looked around. "Where's Benny?"

Henry looked around, too. "I don't know."

A few minutes later, Benny came in from the backyard. There was a smudge of dirt on his nose.

"Where were you, Benny?" Jessie wanted to know.

"I was on a top-secret mission," Benny said mysteriously. "But I can't tell you about it just yet."

The other Aldens looked at one other. What was their little brother up to?

CHAPTER 6

Uh-oh!

When the Aldens came downstairs the next morning, a pancake breakfast was waiting for them. Aunt Jane was having a cup of coffee and reading the paper. She looked up as the children came into the room.

"You're not going to believe what's in the paper," she said, shaking her head.

The Aldens were instantly curious. As they crowded around, Aunt Jane read the headline aloud: IS THE TRAP-DOOR THEATER HAUNTED?

"Oh, no!" Violet cried.

Over breakfast, Aunt Jane read the article to them. It was all about the strange things that had been happening at the theater. It finished with the story of the spilled popcorn—and the spotlight shining on the first row.

"I don't get it." Henry lifted a sausage onto his plate. "We cleared all the popcorn away before anybody saw it. How did the newspaper find out?"

"I suppose somebody leaked it to them," said Aunt Jane.

"But we were the only ones who knew about it," Benny insisted, pouring syrup over his stack of pancakes.

"You're forgetting about Ray," Henry reminded them.

"Oh, right." Benny licked a drop of syrup from the back of his hand.

"You think Ray told the paper?" Violet wondered.

Henry nodded. "That'd be my guess. After all, he said they wouldn't do a write-up on the theater—unless it was sure to grab the readers' attention."

"But . . . will people still will buy tickets?" Benny wanted to know.

Aunt Jane sighed. "It could go either way."

"Either way?" Benny repeated, not understanding.

"The Trap-Door Theater just made front-page news," said Aunt Jane.

Henry understood what she meant. "Some people might think this is good publicity."

Aunt Jane nodded. "Only time will tell if it brings folks into the theater or—"

"Scares them away," finished Violet.

Everyone was unusually quiet as they ate breakfast. They were lost in thought about the mystery. It wasn't until they stepped outside that Benny spoke up.

"Come on!" he said, breaking into a run. "Come and see what I made."

Henry, Jessie, and Violet hurried across the yard behind Benny. They came to a stop outside the shed.

"It's a mold of the prowler's footprint," Benny told them proudly.

Sure enough, a shoeprint in the dirt had been filled with plaster.

"So that's what you were up to yesterday!" Jessie realized.

Benny nodded, beaming. "Now we can figure out who stole the box of tapes."

"That's good detective work, Benny," Henry said, taking a closer look at the mold. "There's only one problem . . . a prowler didn't make this footprint."

"How can you be sure?" Jessie asked.

Henry pulled off his sneaker. "Take a look at the tread on the bottom of my shoe."

"Oh!" cried Violet. "It matches the markings in the plaster."

Benny's jaw dropped. "But . . . "

"I stepped in the mud yesterday," Henry explained, "when I came out to get Alice's appointment book for Aunt Jane."

"That can't be your shoeprint, Henry," Benny insisted. "See? The mold's too small for your shoe."

"Benny's right," Violet said.

"There's a reason for that," Henry said.

"The footprint was made when the ground was still wet from the rain. Remember what Ray told us? A footprint shrinks when the sun dries up the mud."

"Oh, right. And Benny made the mold after the sun had been out all day," Jessie realized.

Benny's shoulders slumped. He looked crushed. Violet felt her little brother's disappointment. "Never mind," she said, as they walked their bikes across the yard. "It was a good try."

"It sure was," agreed Jessie. "Nobody else even thought of looking for footprints."

Benny brightened. "Good detectives always think of stuff like that."

"Come on, Benny," Henry said, giving his brother a playful nudge. "We've got posters to put up." With that, the four Aldens pedaled away.

When they arrived at the Trap-Door Theater, they spotted Ray giving directions to the crew on stage. As the children came down the aisle, the director looked up and gave them a friendly wave.

"Be right with you, kids!" he called out. "Why don't you take a seat for a minute?"

"Ray won't be very happy when he finds out about the missing tape recorder," Henry said, as they sat down in the front row.

"And the missing tapes," added Jessie.

Benny, who was bending over to tie up his shoe, suddenly said, "That's funny."

"What's is it, Benny?" Jessie asked.

"There's something under my seat."

The others looked over as Benny pulled out a wooden box.

"Is that what I think it is?" Violet asked in disbelief.

As Benny lifted the lid, they all stared wide-eyed at Alice's tapes.

"Look," said Jessie. "The tape recorder's in there, too."

"Uh-oh!" Benny's eyes were huge. "I bet I'm sitting in Alice Duncan's seat!"

Just then, Ray hurried over with the posters. "Sorry to keep you waiting. These are the last of the posters." He looked surprised

when he spotted the tapes on Benny's lap. "I see you brought the whole box with you. Actually, I only needed the tape recorder."

"We didn't bring the box with us, Ray," Jessie said, handing him the tape recorder as he handed her the posters. "Somebody stole the tapes from Aunt Jane's shed."

Ray looked confused. "Isn't that the box of tapes on Benny's lap?"

"Yes," said Henry. "But Benny just found it."

"What?" Ray laughed a little. "You're kidding, right?"

"It was under my seat," Benny told him.

"But . . . how did that happen?" asked Ray.

Henry shrugged. "I guess it's another practical joke."

Ray stared at the box of tapes. Then he turned on his heel and quickly walked away.

"That was odd," said Violet. "It's just another prank, right? I wonder why Ray looked so shocked."

Benny shrugged. "It doesn't make sense."

"Nothing about this mystery makes sense," said Henry.

Nobody could argue with that.

CHAPTER 7

A Shrinking Footprint

At the dress rehearsal that evening, the Aldens sat in the audience with Aunt Jane and Ray Shaw. The play was full of suspense—the children watched as Lady Chadwick tracked down clues to find the thief of a priceless diamond necklace. In the final act, with all the suspects gathered together, Lady Chadwick summed up the case. "I came across a footprint in the dried mud," she said. "After making a plaster mold of the print, I soon discovered it fit someone's shoe exactly. In fact, the thief is in this very room. I believe the butler did it!"

The Aldens suddenly looked at one another in surprise. "Did you hear that?" whispered Benny.

"Yes," Jessie whispered back. "There's a mistake in the play!"

Henry nodded. "If Lady Chadwick made the mold when the mud was dry—"

"The footprint would've shrunk!" finished Violet.

Jessie agreed. "It would never fit the butler's shoe exactly."

As the curtain went down, Aunt Jane turned to the director. "What a wonderful play!" she said, clapping along with the children. Ray looked pleased. "I just hope it goes half as well on opening night."

Backstage, they found everyone gathered together in one of the dressing rooms. The cast and crew were helping themselves to the hot and cold food set out on a long table. The children followed the line of people slowly around the table while Aunt Jane went over to congratulate Fern Robson.

After helping themselves to the different dishes, the Aldens sat down in a corner with their heaping plates. "Did you get some of Aunt Jane's sweet-and-sour meatballs, Benny?" Violet asked. "They're really good."

Benny nodded as he crunched into a pickle. "Should we tell Ray?" he asked. "About the footprint, I mean."

"Let's hold off on that for now," Jessie suggested, as she looked around at all the smiling faces.

Henry was quick to agree. "Everybody's having such a good time. It'd be a shame to spoil it."

Just then, something caught Violet's eye. "Don't all look at once," she said, "but isn't that Gil Diggs talking to Ray?"

One by one, the other Aldens looked over. "That's Gil, all right," Jessie said in surprise. "I wonder what he's doing here?"

"Beats me," said Henry. "He's not exactly a big fan of the Trap-Door Theater."

A moment later, Aunt Jane sat down beside

Benny. "I was just having a chat with Gil," she said. "Guess what he told me?"

The children were instantly curious. "What was it, Aunt Jane?"

"He's planning to turn his movie theater into a children's playhouse!"

Benny's eyebrows shot up. "A playhouse?" he echoed. "You mean, like our boxcar?"

Aunt Jane smiled a little. "Not exactly, Benny. Instead of showing movies in his theater, he'll be putting on plays for children."

"That's not a bad idea," Henry said, thoughtfully.

"Gil stopped by to get some pointers from Ray," Aunt Jane explained. "Apparently, he got a loan from the bank. Of course," she added, "it'll mean shutting his theater down for a while to build a stage. But Gil thinks it'll be worth it."

Jessie suddenly understood. *That's* what Gil had meant on the phone: he was talking about shutting down his own theater!

The Aldens looked at one another. They were each thinking the same thing.

They could cross Gil Diggs off their list of suspects.

"Ah, there you are, Jane!" Ray hurried over with Tricia Jenkins. "I wanted to introduce you to our contest winner."

Aunt Jane held out her hand. "So nice to meet you, Tricia. I don't know when I've enjoyed a play more," she said with a warm smile. "By the way, do you know the children? This is Henry and—"

"We've met," Tricia broke in, barely looking over.

Jessie and Henry exchanged glances. It was clear Tricia wasn't pleased to see them again.

"That surprise twist in the last act was brilliant," Aunt Jane went on. "I never saw it coming!"

Ray nodded approvingly. "Tricia has a real gift for keeping an audience on the edge of their seats. Right, Fern?" he added, as the actress joined their group.

"Yes, it's a wonderful play," Fern agreed, looking over at the author. "One thing, though, Tricia. I always try to understand the character I'm playing. Maybe you could shed some light on Lady Chadwick's hat."

Tricia blinked in surprise. "What are you talking about?"

"I'm talking about the flowers," said Fern. "It must mean something that Lady Chadwick wears them on her hat."

"It means she likes carnations." Tricia shrugged. "It's as simple as that."

"You mean marigolds," Fern said. "Those are yellow marigolds on her hat."

"No, they're carnations, aren't they?" Tricia argued.

"Marigolds," Fern said, shaking her head.

"Well . . . whatever," said Tricia, shrugging.

"I'm surprised at you, Tricia," Fern told her. "You underlined 'yellow marigolds' in your script. How could you forget?"

"Honestly, Fern!" Tricia snapped. "Why do you have to make such a big deal out of everything? Lady Chadwick is fond of yellow marigolds. End of story."

Jessie caught Henry's eye. Why was Tricia

getting so upset?

"Alice Duncan liked them, too," Benny was saying. "Yellow marigolds, I mean."

Tricia seemed startled by Benny's remark. "I'm afraid I wouldn't know about that," she said, fiddling nervously with her necklace. "I never had the pleasure of meeting Alice Duncan."

Violet couldn't help noticing the gold heart on the chain around Tricia's neck. The heart was engraved with the letters *P.J.* Something seemed oddly familiar about the initials. But Violet couldn't quite put her finger on what it was.

"Well, I think Alice would be very pleased if she knew yellow marigolds appeared in the winning play," Aunt Jane remarked. "They were her favorite flower."

Ray chuckled. "Alice was quite a character, wasn't she? And how about that old typewriter of hers? Now, there's a real antique!"

Aunt Jane nodded. "The keys kept sticking, but that never stopped Alice."

"I prefer a computer, myself," Tricia said,

her voice cold. "I can't imagine using an old typewriter that doesn't print *w* at all." With that, she turned and walked away.

Jessie stared after her, puzzled. Nobody had mentioned the typewriter wouldn't print *w*. How did Tricia know?

CHAPTER 8

Something Smells Fishy

"We should tell Ray about the footprint," Benny insisted, as they worked in Aunt Jane's vegetable garden the next day.

"I think so, too," said Jessie, shaking the dirt from the roots of a weed. Henry nodded. "We'll tell Ray about it the next time we see him."

"I'm sure it'd be easy enough to change the script," Violet added.

Henry sat down on a rock. "Wow, that afternoon sun sure is getting hot," he said.

"I vote we cool off in the pond."

"I second that!" said Jessie. "Let's clean up here, then we can change into our swim suits."

As they put the garden tools away in the shed, Henry noticed that Jessie's gaze was fixed on the old typewriter.

"What is it, Jessie?" he asked.

"I was just wondering how Tricia knew about Alice's typewriter," she said. "That it wouldn't print *w* at all, I mean. I'm sure no one mentioned it."

Henry, Violet, and Benny had thought nothing of it. But now they wondered about it, too.

"That is weird," said Violet.

Jessie nodded. "Tricia must have met Alice."

"Do you think she told a lie?" Benny wanted to know.

"I doubt it," said Henry, "and I'll tell you why. If she had been a friend of Alice's, Aunt Jane would have met her before last night."

"Good point," said Jessie, as they stepped

outside. "Aunt Jane said she knew all of Alice's friends."

"Not all," Benny argued. "Aunt Jane didn't know P.J."

"Who?" Jessie looked puzzled, but only for a moment. "Oh, you mean the friend in Alice's appointment book."

Violet suddenly whirled around. "That's it!"

"What's it?" Benny wanted to know.

"I knew there was something familiar about the initials on Tricia's necklace," Violet explained, her voice rising with excitement. "The letters *p* and *j* were engraved on the gold heart she was wearing."

Benny scratched his head. "But . . . Tricia's name begins with a *t*, doesn't it?"

"Yes, but Patricia starts with a *p*," Violet pointed out.

"Oh, I get it!" cried Benny, catching on. "Tricia is short for Patricia."

Violet nodded. "I have a hunch Tricia is P.J."

"If you're right, Violet," said Jessie, "then

Tricia really did lie about not knowing Alice."

Benny frowned. "I wonder why she'd do something like that?"

"Beats me!" Henry shrugged. "I think I'm too hot to think straight right now."

With that, they hurried off to change into their swim suits. For a while, they put all thoughts of the mystery aside as they splashed about in the pond near their aunt's house. It wasn't until they were heading back across the clover fields, towels flung over their shoulders, that Jessie suddenly snapped her fingers.

"Tricia isn't the only nickname for Patricia!" she cried.

Henry stopped. "What are you talking about, Jessie?"

"Remember that ad for a typist? The one that fell out of Alice's appointment book."

Henry nodded. So did Violet and Benny.

"What was the name in the ad?" Jessie asked.

Henry thought for a moment. "Wasn't it Patty?"

"Exactly," said Jessie. "And Patty is another nickname for—"

"Patricia!" cried Violet, in sudden understanding.

This got Henry thinking. "Tricia *did* change her nickname," he recalled. "At least, that's what Ray said."

"Maybe she thought Tricia had more pizzazz than Patty," guessed Benny.

"Wait a minute," said Violet. "Are you saying it was Tricia's ad in the paper?"

"I'm not a hundred percent sure," Jessie answered. "But it's possible Tricia and Patty are the same person."

"Then that would mean Alice hired Tricia to type up her plays," Henry concluded.

They had to admit it was possible. Didn't Aunt Jane say that Alice hired a college student? And didn't Tricia earn money for school on her computer?

"I don't get it." Benny frowned. "Why would Tricia lie about it?"

"That's a good question, Benny," said Henry.

"We can't be sure Tricia and Patty are the same person," Violet pointed out.

"You're right," Jessie was forced to admit.

"I guess there's no way of proving it," added Henry.

"I know a way," cried Benny, racing ahead. He called back over his shoulder, "Come on!"

As soon as they got back to the house, the youngest Alden headed straight for Alice's appointment book. When he gave it a shake, the ad fell out onto the kitchen table.

"What's up?" Henry asked, trying to catch his breath.

Benny handed him the newspaper clipping. "I think we should call this number."

Henry slapped his brother a high-five. "You're a genius!"

Benny grinned. "I guess I am."

Jessie, Violet, and Benny gathered around as Henry dialed the number in the ad. He held the receiver up so they could all listen. With their heads close together, they heard the message on the answering machine: "Hi,

you've reached Patty. Please leave a message and I'll return your call as soon as possible."

"There's no doubt about it," Jessie said, as Henry hung up. "That was Tricia's voice."

"This is getting stranger and stranger," said Benny.

"It sure is." Violet poured lemonade into four tall glasses. "If Tricia was hired to type Alice's plays, why would she keep it a secret? There's nothing wrong with helping Alice, is there?"

"No," said Henry. "Not if that's all it was."

"You think there's more to it than that?" Violet wondered.

"Got to be." Henry sounded very sure. "Why else would Tricia want to keep it a secret?"

Nobody said anything for a while. They were all deep in thought as they sat around the kitchen table, sipping lemonade.

"It does seem strange," Jessie said at last. "It's almost as if Tricia's hiding something."

"That's not all that's strange," said Henry,

who was staring at the last entry in Alice's appointment book.

Benny was swirling the ice cubes in his glass. "What is it, Henry?" he asked.

"There's something weird about this last entry."

"What's weird about it, Henry?" Benny wanted to know. "Alice bought shoes that didn't fit. You said that yourself the other day."

"I said that then. Now I'm not so sure."

"What are you thinking, Henry?" Violet wondered.

"Alice didn't write 'shoes won't fit'—she wrote *'shoe* won't fit.'"

Jessie inched her chair closer. "You're right," she said, glancing at the appointment book. "It *does* say shoe—not shoes." She looked from Henry to the entry and back again. "That is a bit weird."

Henry said, "Maybe this entry has nothing to do with returning a pair of shoes."

"What else could it mean?" Violet wanted to know.

Henry paused for a moment to sort out his thoughts. "What if Alice was talking about the butler's shoe?"

Benny blinked in surprise. "Alice had a butler?"

"No, no." Henry smiled a little at this. "I'm talking about Lady Chadwick's butler."

"What are you saying, Henry?" Jessie asked.

"What if Alice noticed the mistake in the play?" said Henry. "Maybe she realized the butler's shoe wouldn't fit a mold that was made in dried mud."

"You think Alice wanted P.J.—Tricia—to make a change to the script?" Violet asked, after a moment's thought.

"I'm only guessing," said Henry. "But I think it's possible."

"If you're right," Jessie concluded, "then Alice must've read Tricia's play."

Violet thought about this. "Maybe Alice was giving her a few pointers."

"Could be," said Henry. "But why would Tricia keep it a secret? That's the part I don't get."

Violet nodded. "There's something here we're not understanding."

"I don't know what to make of it either," said Jessie. "Unless . . . "

"Unless what?" asked Benny.

Jessie's mind was racing. "I keep thinking about Lady Chadwick's hat."

"That it was hanging from the chandelier in the lobby?" said Benny. "Is that what you mean, Jessie?"

"No, it's not that."

"What then?" asked Henry.

"I'm talking about the yellow marigolds," said Jessie. "Don't you think it's odd Tricia didn't remember what kind of flowers Lady Chadwick was wearing?"

Benny nodded. "She called them carnations."

"Exactly," said Jessie. "And yet, she underlined 'yellow marigolds' in the script. At least, that's what Fern said."

Henry was curious. "Where are you going with this, Jessie?"

"Yellow marigolds were Alice's favorite

flower," Jessie reminded them, hoping they would understand what she was driving at. Seeing their puzzled faces, she added, "Alice always put yellow marigolds in her plays."

"You think it's more than just a coincidence?" Violet wondered. "That Tricia put yellow marigolds in her play, too, I mean."

Jessie nodded her head slowly. "I think it's a lot more than just a coincidence."

"Back up a minute, Jessie," Henry put in. "Are you saying Alice noticed a mistake—in her own play?"

"That's exactly what I'm saying," Jessie told him. "It's possible she wanted to make the change before Tricia typed up the last act."

Violet's eyes widened. "You really think Alice Duncan wrote *Lady Chadwick's Riddle?*"

"If she did . . . that means—" began Benny.

Henry cut in. "It means Tricia put her name on Alice's play."

"Oh!" Violet put her hand over her mouth. "You don't really think Tricia would do something so terrible, do you?"

"I don't want to believe it, Violet," said Jessie. "But it's a pretty strong case against Tricia."

Henry agreed. "It would explain why Tricia lied about knowing Alice."

"And she could easily have put her name on Lady Chadwick's Riddle after Alice died," Jessie pointed out.

"But why would Tricia do something like that?" Violet wondered.

Henry shrugged. "Maybe she saw the contest as a way to make some quick cash."

Benny was thinking. "I bet Tricia stole Alice's tapes, too."

"You might be on to something, Benny," Henry had to admit. "Chances are, she wanted to make sure there wasn't another copy of Alice's play."

"Still," said Violet, "I don't think we should jump to any conclusions."

Henry nodded. "You're right, Violet. It's one thing to suspect someone. It's another thing to have proof."

"But we can't just do nothing," Benny insisted. "Can we?"

"It wouldn't hurt to ask a few questions," Henry said after a moment's thought. "Aunt Jane has some errands to run in town. Maybe we could get a ride with her to the theater."

The Aldens weren't sure what they were going to do. They only knew they had to do something.

CHAPTER 9

Pointing a Finger

As they pulled up in front of the Trap-Door Theater, Aunt Jane glanced at her watch. "I'll get my errands done, then meet you back here."

"Perfect!" said Henry, as they climbed out of the car.

Aunt Jane gave them a little wave, then drove away.

Violet slowed her step. "What if we're wrong?" She was having second thoughts about their suspicions.

"Grandfather says we're seldom wrong when it comes to hunches," Benny reminded her.

"And if we're right," added Jessie, "we can't let Tricia get away with stealing Alice's play, can we?"

Henry held the theater door open. "Don't worry, Violet," he said. "We'll just ask a few questions and see how Tricia reacts."

"That sounds fair," agreed Violet.

Inside the theater, the Aldens hurried backstage where preparations for opening night were in full swing. Stagehands were rushing about, testing the lights and setting up props. As the children passed an opened door, a familiar voice called out to them.

"The Aldens!"

Ray, who was sitting at his desk, motioned for them to come in. Across from him, Tricia Jenkins and Fern Robson had their heads bent over their scripts.

"Did you forget we're out of posters?" Ray asked, smiling as the children stepped into his office.

"No, we didn't forget," Henry told him. "We were hoping you might have time to talk. It's about Alice Duncan."

Tricia suddenly glanced up from her script. A look of shock crossed her face, but only for a moment. She quickly pulled herself together. "We're in the middle of a script meeting," she said, making a shooing motion with her hand. "The play opens tomorrow night. We don't have time to chat."

"Speak for yourself." Fern frowned over at Tricia. "I could use a break."

"Let's take five," Ray suggested. He put his feet up on his desk and leaned back with his hands behind his head. "What's up, kids?"

The Aldens looked at one other. They weren't really sure how to begin. Finally, Violet spoke up.

"The thing is," she said in a quiet voice, "we noticed a mistake in the play."

Jessie nodded. "We thought we should mention it."

Tricia looked amused. "Well, aren't we lucky we have the Aldens around to give us a few pointers," she said, though it was clear from her voice that she didn't think they were lucky at all.

Henry squared his shoulders. "It's true," he insisted. "There's a mistake in the last act." He reminded Ray of what he'd told them—that a footprint shrinks after the sun dries up the mud. Henry finished by saying, "If Lady Chadwick made the mold when the mud was dry, the butler's shoe would never fit exactly."

"Of course!" said Ray. "How could I miss that?" He shook his head. "Looks like we'll be making a change to the script."

Tricia stiffened. "No one pays attention to that stuff. Do you honestly think anyone will notice?"

"The Aldens did," Ray reminded her.

"And so did Alice Duncan!" Benny blurted out.

Henry and Jessie exchanged glances. There was no going back now. They could only hope they were on the right track.

"Alice Duncan noticed?" Fern's mouth

dropped open. "That's strange."

"Not as strange as you might think," Jessie told her. "You see, Alice made one last entry in her appointment book before she died."

"Yes, I remember seeing it." Ray nodded his head slowly. "Something about returning a pair of shoes, wasn't it?"

"That's what we thought, too," said Henry. "At first."

"And now?"

"Now we think Alice realized there was a mistake in the last act of Lady Chadwick's Riddle," said Violet. "That's why she wrote, 'Shoe won't fit. Tell P.J. to make change.'"

"P.J.?" Fern looked over at Tricia suspiciously. "Patricia Jenkins?"

"Hang on a minute!" Ray put up a hand. "How would *Alice* know anything about a mistake in *your* play, Tricia?"

Tricia swallowed hard. Everyone's eyes were fixed on her. Finally, she cleared her throat and said, "Alice Duncan was giving me advice on my play. What's wrong with that?"

"Why would Alice give advice to someone she didn't know?" demanded Henry.

It was a good question. Tricia said she'd never met Alice. Everyone waited expectantly for an answer.

"I never actually met Alice," said Tricia. "But I did send my play to her in the mail."

The children looked at each another. Tricia seemed to have an answer for everything. But Henry wasn't giving up so easily.

"Are you sure there wasn't more to it than that?" he asked, giving Tricia a meaningful look.

"What are you saying?" Tricia snapped. "You can't prove I've done anything dishonest."

Ray's eyes narrowed as he looked over at Tricia. But he didn't say anything.

"I bet a tape of Alice's play would prove it," Benny said, his hands on his hips.

"What?" Tricia shifted nervously. "But . . . I . . . I checked every one of those tapes and—" She stopped abruptly as if realizing she'd said too much.

Henry and Jessie looked at each other in surprise. Benny's remark had only been wishful thinking. Had Tricia misunderstood? Did she think they actually had Alice's voice on tape—recording *Lady Chadwick's Riddle?*

Benny looked Tricia straight in the eye. "You stole the box of tapes from Aunt Jane's shed, didn't you?"

"That's ridiculous!" Tricia forced a tense laugh. "Why would I do something like that?"

Henry spoke up. "You wanted to make sure there wasn't another copy of *Lady Chadwick's Riddle.*"

"What's this all about, kids?" asked Ray, who was pacing around the room. "Surely you're not suggesting Tricia stole Alice Duncan's play?"

When she heard this, Fern's jaw dropped. She was too shocked to speak.

"What do you have to say for yourself, Tricia?" Ray asked.

Tricia opened her mouth several times as if about to speak, then closed it again. Finally, she sank back in her chair, looking defeated. "It's true," she confessed, burying her head in her hands. "I signed my name to Alice Duncan's play."

"What?" Ray stopped pacing. "How could you do such a thing?"

"I knew it was wrong," Tricia admitted, "but when I heard about the contest, I decided to enter Alice's play." She lifted her head. "The funny thing is, I really didn't believe *Lady Chadwick's Riddle* would win."

Jessie guessed what was coming next. "When it did, you decided to keep the cash."

Tricia didn't deny it. "I've always had to work so hard to put myself through school."

Ray looked at her, stunned. "That doesn't make it okay to steal."

"How did you get hold of Alice's play in the first place?" Fern wanted to know.

Violet turned to Tricia. "Alice hired you to type her plays, didn't she?"

Tricia nodded. "I was finishing up the last act of *Lady Chadwick's Riddle* when Alice died.

I figured if I put my name on the play, nobody would ever catch on. I really couldn't see the harm," she added, trying to make light of it. "After all, Alice would finally have a play performed in public."

"And you could take the credit for it," finished Fern.

"And the cash," added Jessie.

"There was only one problem," said Ray. "You hadn't counted on the Aldens coming along and figuring everything out."

Tricia had to admit this was true. "I thought it was a foolproof plan, Ray. At least, until I overheard you talking about Alice's tape recorder. You said it was in the box with her tapes. That's when it suddenly hit me that Alice might have made an extra copy of her play."

"So you went out to Aunt Jane's on that rainy night," Benny said. "And you took the tapes from the shed. I saw you."

"Yes, I did," Tricia confessed. "I checked every one of those tapes, but I couldn't find another copy of *Lady Chadwick's Riddle*."

"That's because there isn't another copy," Jessie informed her.

"You . . . you don't really have Alice's voice on tape?" Tricia's shoulders slumped. "I can't believe I fell for your bluff."

"You almost got away with it, Tricia," Ray realized. Then he added, "You left the box of tapes under a seat in the first row, didn't you?"

Tricia nodded. "I figured everyone would think it was just another prank."

"Let me get this straight," said Fern, her eyes flashing. "You're the one who staged all those ghostly pranks?"

"No!" Tricia cried. "I took Alice's tapes, but that's all. I had nothing to do with anything else."

The Aldens exchanged looks. Was Tricia telling the truth?

"I can't believe you took credit for someone else's work," said Ray. "How could you tell such a lie?" He sounded more disappointed than angry.

Tricia looked at the floor. "I wish I could

go back and undo what I've done," she said, her voice shaking. "I'm so sorry."

"Sorry isn't enough," Ray told her, his face grim. "You'll have to return the prize money, Tricia. And it'll be a long time before anyone will trust you again."

With that, Tricia walked slowly from the room, looking truly regretful.

CHAPTER 10

Taking a Bow

"I just can't believe it," Ray told Aunt Jane and the Aldens on opening night. They were gathered in Fern's dressing room during intermission. "Tickets have been selling like hotcakes!"

"Isn't it wonderful?" said Fern, who was sitting at her dressing table. "The play's sold out right through the summer!" She pulled out a tissue and blotted her lipstick.

Violet's eyes were shining. "That's great news!"

"When the truth came out about Tricia Jenkins," said Ray, "I was afraid nobody would come near the theater."

"That worried me, too." Aunt Jane nodded. "But, thank goodness, the newspaper put a great spin on everything."

The Aldens grinned as Henry pointed to the headline: TWO MYSTERIES FOR THE PRICE OF ONE!

The report described how Tricia tried to steal Alice Duncan's play—and how the Aldens had pieced together clues and cracked the case.

Fern powdered her nose. "That article really caught the public's interest."

But the children knew the mystery wasn't fully explained. They still weren't sure who was behind all the ghostly pranks at the theater.

Henry had a question. "There's something I don't understand, Fern. If you really believed the theater was haunted, why did you keep coming here?"

"Oh, it wasn't easy, Henry," Fern told him. "I even broke out in a nervous rash. See?"

She pushed up her sleeve. "But you know what they say—the show must go on!"

Henry looked at Jessie. Jessie nodded. Fern really believed the theater was haunted. It wasn't just an act.

"I knew you wouldn't let everyone down, Fern," said Ray. "And you must admit, we sure got some good publicity out of those ghostly pranks."

"Is that why you told the newspaper about the popcorn, Ray?" asked Henry.

"Yes." Ray nodded. "When I met the reporter—that morning at the diner—I told him everything. I figured I'd give him something worth writing about. I didn't want the article buried somewhere in the back pages. And it did the trick, too," he added proudly. "That story made front-page news."

Benny, who had been listening with a puzzled frown, suddenly spoke up. "But you met with the reporter before we even saw the spilled popcorn."

The Aldens looked at each other. Something didn't add up. How could Ray mention something he hadn't even seen?

"Well, I, um . . . " Ray struggled to find something to say. Then he took a deep breath and said, "I guess you found me out."

"What are you saying, Ray?" Aunt Jane looked puzzled.

"I'm saying I was behind all those practical jokes."

"What?" Fern stared at the director. She paused as if she couldn't quite believe what she had heard. "You tried to scare me?"

"It's not what you think, Fern," Ray told her. "I never meant to scare you. I even made sure you wouldn't be at the theater to see the spilled popcorn."

"That's why you wanted Fern to get her beauty sleep that morning," guessed Jessie.

"But why?" Aunt Jane questioned. "Why would you try to fool everyone?"

"I love my job," Ray said. "And I was afraid I'd lose it if the theater shut down."

"I don't understand." Aunt Jane shook her head in bewilderment. "What does that have to do with fooling everyone?"

Henry was ready with an answer. "It was a publicity stunt, wasn't it?"

"Yes, I thought it'd make headlines—and it did." Ray shrugged a little. "So there you have it. I'm guilty as charged."

"Honestly, Ray!" Fern rolled her eyes. "Alice wrote a brilliant play. Tickets would've sold without any help from you."

"And Fern's wowing the audience," put in Aunt Jane.

Ray couldn't argue. "You're right," he said. "We didn't need gimmicks to drum up ticket sales. I know that now."

"You did everything then?" asked Benny, who still couldn't get over it. "The popcorn, the hat hanging from the chandelier, the—"

"Not quite everything," Ray corrected. "I wasn't responsible for the missing tapes. That was all Tricia's doing."

Jessie nodded. "No wonder you looked so shocked when Benny found the tapes under his seat."

"I knew I hadn't put them there," Ray said, chuckling to himself. "It had me wondering if the theater really was haunted."

"I guess you got a taste of your own medicine." Fern gave him a sideways glance. "Didn't you, Ray?"

"Yes, I guess I did." Ray turned to the actress. "Can you ever forgive me for what I've done, Fern?" he asked sheepishly.

Fern folded her arms in front of her and looked away without answering.

"Come on," Ray pleaded. "Don't be like that."

"For the life of me," Fern said, shaking her head, "I don't know why I should forgive you." Then a slow smile began to curl her lips. "But . . . all's well that ends well, I suppose," she said, softening a little.

Just then, there was a knock at the door. A muffled voice announced, "Two minutes, Miss Robson."

While Aunt Jane and the Aldens watched the rest of the play from the wings, Ray whispered, "I'm glad the truth is out about those pranks. It's a load off my mind."

"The truth is out about Alice Duncan,

too," added Aunt Jane. "Now everybody knows who really won the contest."

"Thanks to the Aldens!" said Ray.

When the curtain went down, Aunt Jane turned to the director. "I think you have a real hit on your hands," she said, while a thunder of applause filled the theater.

As Fern took a bow, she gestured for the Aldens to join her on center stage.

"That's your cue, kids," Ray said, urging them on.

The four children came out from the wings just as Fern announced, "I give you . . . Henry, Jessie, Violet, and Benny!"

With the audience cheering, the Aldens took a bow.

GERTRUDE CHANDLER WARNER discovered when she was teaching that many readers who like an exciting story could find no books that were both easy and fun to read. She decided to try to meet this need, and her first book, *The Boxcar Children*, quickly proved she had succeeded.

Miss Warner drew on her own experiences to write the mystery. As a child she spent hours watching trains go by on the tracks opposite her family home. She often dreamed about what it would be like to set up housekeeping in a caboose or freight car — the situation the Alden children find themselves in.

While the mystery element is central to each of Miss Warner's books, she never thought of them as strictly juvenile mysteries. She liked to stress the Aldens' independence and resourcefulness and their solid New England devotion to using up and making do. The Aldens go about most of their adventures with as little adult supervision as possible — something else that delights young readers.

Miss Warner lived in Putnam, Connecticut, until her death in 1979. During her lifetime, she received hundreds of letters from girls and boys telling her how much they liked her books.